Ju
F
T49   Tinbergen, Niko.
            Kleew: the story of a
        gull.

Kleew

*K*leew

THE STORY OF A GULL

BY

NIKOLAAS TINBERGEN

Lyons & Burford

PUBLISHERS

Printed in the United States of America
10 9 8 7 6 5 4 3 2 1

LIBRARY OF CONGRESS
CATALOGING-IN-PUBLICATION
DATA

Tinbergen, Niko, 1907–
Kleew : the story of a gull / by Nikolaas
Tinbergen.
p. cm.
Reprint. Originally published: New York:
Oxford University Press, c1947.
Summary: The seagull Kleew and his mate Klia
grow from hatchlings, learn to fly, tolerate
curious humans, and eventually build a nest
and raise youngsters of their own.
ISBN 1-55821-122-5
1. Gulls—Juvenile fiction. [1.
Gulls—Fiction.]
I. Title.
PZ10.3.T45K1 1991
[Fic]—dc20
91-15867 CIP AC

Kleew is a gull. His father and his mother live on the top of a high sand dune in Holland. From there they can see the ocean. Now and then they fly to the ocean to get their food. They find it on the shore. It is mostly dead animals, washed up by the waves—small fish, mussels, or crabs. Gulls like these much more than bread, or cereal, or even candy.

Kleew is a very small gull. In fact he isn't even a gull yet. Not even a chick. He is still an egg. His little brother and sister are eggs, too. Each egg is a kind of house, for in them the chicks are living. Together the eggs lie in the nest on top of the dune where their father and mother are living.

The father and mother gull take turns sitting on the eggs to keep them warm, so that the chicks inside can grow. They grow so fast that the egg soon becomes too narrow for them. They wonder how they can break the eggs and get out.

3

All at once Kleew feels that his bill touches the hard shell of the egg. He pushes and pushes, and . . . crack! He has made a little crack in the shell. He pushes again—crack, and now there is a real hole. Look at the picture, you can see Kleew's bill through the opening. On top of his bill is a sharp little nail. That is what he cracked the shell with.

Now he is able to breathe through the hole, and he can also make faint squeaks. He goes on pushing. He widens the hole. Suddenly the shell bursts open, and look, Kleew tumbles out of his egg! What a queer little fellow! He is all wet. He closes his eyes for he is not used to daylight, and he is panting. That is because he has been working so hard.

His mother takes him under her wings to keep him nice and warm. Kleew must wait till his sleek wet coat dries. See, at the end of the day when his mother gets up, Kleew is no longer a wet, ugly little creature, but a nice downy chick. Very soon he gets on his feet and even walks a few steps. Imagine a one-day-old baby

that can walk! He feels very important. He is a gull though still a very little one who cannot yet fly.

4

Kleew is tired. It is hard work breaking out of an egg. He needs a good rest. He lies very quietly in the warm nest, with his brother, Bill, and his sister, Mary, who have broken through their shells, too. Mother Gull stands nearby. She is resting too, for she also is tired. Three children arriving at once has been very exciting.

After their rest Kleew, Bill and Mary look around. Isn't the world interesting? They can see many other gulls. They are standing near their own nests. There comes Father Gull, high up in the air. He glides and glides, lower and lower, and finally lights near his children. Suddenly Kleew realizes how hungry he is. Hasn't Father something for him to eat?

He rushes toward his father, squeaks as hard as he can, leaps and jumps up and down, and even flaps his wings. Of course they are still tiny wings and no good for flying, but his father seems to understand what Kleew means. At least he produces a fine fat crab which he has kept in his stomach all this time, which is his safe, handy way of keeping things. After all, a gull has no hands! He puts the crab down on the sand. It looks tantalizing to Kleew. His father tears a tidbit from the crab's flesh and takes it in the tip of his bill. But he does not eat it himself. Suddenly Kleew understands that this is for him, that he may eat it. For the first time in his life he is really eating—and a delicious piece of crab meat at that! He eats and eats until he can't hold any more.

6

Every day Kleew got several good square meals. Sometimes it was Father Gull who brought the food, sometimes Mother. Kleew and Mary and Bill grew and grew. In a few days they were so strong that they could crawl out of the nest and even walk around the neighborhood.

When it rained Mother Gull kept them dry under her wings and when the sun came out they liked to feel its warmth on their backs.

One day as they were playing together their mother gave a horrifying cry. At the same instant she flew up in the air. She was very much frightened. The chicks were scared, too. "Kakakakakaka!" Mother cried. "Kakakakaka." That meant, "Watch out children, watch out! Here comes a dog. If he finds you he'll eat you!"

Kleew did not know what a dog was but he understood at once that it must be a very dangerous beast. Kleew ran to a little bush and crouched flat on the ground. He looked exactly like a part of the sandy soil. The dark patches on his down might have been dry leaves or gray moss. Mary and Bill crouched, too. There they lay, scared to death and dead still. Surely the dog would not see them!

Mother, together with the other gulls, flew toward the dog. She tried to frighten him by crying loudly and by swooping fiercely down and hitting him with her feet. Kleew, still lying very quietly, looked at her and admired her. Brave Mother! Would the dog be frightened, or would he come still nearer?

Fortunately he went away. Mother returned, laughing happily, and the three chicks dared move again. What a terrible adventure that had been!

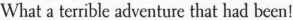

8

One day, while both Father and Mother were away, Kleew saw something strange. High above him in the sky was a soaring bird. It was not a gull. It was dark and not white, it had a funny short neck and a long, long tail. Kleew watched it for a long time. To get a good view of it, he turned his head sidewise and looked at it with one eye, just the way a grown gull would. Luckily, Kleew kept very quiet, for the strange bird was a sparrow hawk and sparrow hawks like to eat young gulls. This one did not see Kleew, though Kleew saw him well enough, and the hawk went on.

Kleew was bored. Also, he was hungry again. If only Mother and Father would come back! He preened his feathers with his bill. Then he yawned. What a huge mouth! Then he flapped his wings, just as if he were about to fly. Do you see how much his wings have been growing?

One day very early in the
morning, it was still dark,
Kleew saw a huge beast coming his way. It was
much larger than the dog and it walked on two legs,
just like Kleew himself. Father and Mother were very
much afraid of the beast so they called again, "Children, watch out! Stay just where you are and don't
move!"

Kleew and Mary and Bill crouched on the ground
and kept very still. The strange giant wandered around
for a long time. Father and Mother were terribly upset.

When the beast left at last it left a very curious
thing behind. It was a tent—Mr. Tinbergen's tent, for
that was the monster's name. He was a man, but
Kleew called him a beast for he had never seen a man.

The three chicks were rather afraid of the tent and
thought it wiser to move away from it. In moving they
came close to the nest of another gull. The other gull
did not want them near
him and all at once made a
charge and chased them
away. How Kleew ran!

For a few days every-
thing was quiet, then something much more horrible
occurred. Mr. Tinbergen
and another man visited
the gulls again. Kleew hid
as well as he could. At last
they found him! They lift-
ed him off the ground and
got hold of one of his legs.
You should have seen how
he fluttered and heard how he cried! But the men only
put a ring around his leg with a number carved on it.

"#107," it read, "Leiden, Holland." Then Mr.
Tinbergen wrote in his notebook: "Kleew is our gull
#107. If we meet him again some day, we will just
look at the number on his ring, and if it is 107 we will
be sure that it is Kleew."

After the men had left, Kleew was alone with his
ring. Again and again he looked at it, and every time he
was very much astonished. "Now what am I supposed
to do with a ring? Why did that beast put a ring on my
leg?" He did not understand it at all. Mother, too,
came and had a look.

However, soon he got
accustomed to it. And it
was not long before Kleew
was rather proud of his
ring.

As the days went by Kleew gathered much experience and became a rather wise little gull. He discovered that there was much of interest around him. See how astonished he looks at that fly. It's a big blue bottle. "Is that something I can eat?" he seems to wonder. That's not for you, Kleew. The fly is much too quick for you. Also the fly is much too small for a bird like Kleew. See how big his gullet is. That's the right size for swallowing a fish, or crab, or star fish, or clam.

Each day Kleew tried to fly. Bill and Mary tried, too. Look how they flap their wings and jump. But it never seems to work and before they know it they find themselves on the ground, rolling over and fluttering their wings. Their wings are still too small of course; they have to grow a lot more before they are strong enough to fly with. Sometimes Kleew got very impatient and annoyed. He wanted so much to fly the way the old gulls did.

One day, as on so many days before, Kleew tried flapping his wings. Suddenly he felt that he was up in the air. He had really flown! For the first time in his life.

"Mother, Mother, look! Kleew is up in the air!" Mary and Bill shouted at once.

But Mother was already with Kleew, watching him and ready to take care of him in case he should fall. All the gulls in the neighborhood rushed up to Kleew. "Well done, Kleew! Smart lad!" they all called. How proud he was!

Once Kleew was able to fly he decided to go to the beach alone and get his own food. He walked along the water's edge and searched for prey. And he found so much! Shells with the slugs still in them, fish, sea-urchins, snails, and many other very tasty bits. In fact he found many more than he could eat.

In one of these trips to the beach Kleew discovered a crab. He was hungry so naturally he decided to eat it. But the crab felt quite differently. It waved its two strong claws, open and ready to bite. Kleew was frightened. He hesitated then said crossly, "Oh never mind, I'll find someone else to eat today."

Another day Kleew found a big double clam on the shore. He tried to break it open and get at the flesh inside. But the shell was hard and would not break.

And then clever Kleew had a very bright idea. He took the clam in his beak, flew high into the air, and dropped it. "Perhaps it will crash on the ground," he thought.

But the shell fell on the soft sand and did not break. That was too much for Kleew. It was beyond him. Look, how amazed he is. Yes, Kleew, you will have to learn that a shell has to be dropped on something hard.

18

That evening it began to blow. During the night, while Kleew was sleeping on the beach, with many other gulls, the breeze became a real gale. What an unpleasant night! The wind pushed Kleew here and there and he could not sleep at all. The hail came rattling down on his head and shoulders.

The next morning, when it got light, the sea looked very strange. There were wild waves and a grayish foam and a roaring noise. Kleew tried to find some food in the surf but the gale blew so much foam in his eyes that he couldn't see anything. So he went back to the beach and settled down among his friends. Together they waited until the wind should drop. With their heads drawn back between their shoulders and their eyes half closed they stood in the sweeping rainstorm, on the bare wet sand. This was no fit life for a gull!

19

But after the gale there was a real feast for the gulls. The waves had washed many kinds of sea food ashore, each one more delicious than the next. Kleew decided that the nicest of all was a stranded dolphin. Here you see him busy with his meal, together with his friends. See the band around his leg? He has been pecking a hole in the dolphin and through it he tears huge pieces of meat and swallows them eagerly.

Most of the gulls are a little afraid of Kleew and are waiting until he is through. Only his sister, Mary, is allowed to join him. In the meantime the others are quarreling. See those with big black wings? They are black-backed gulls.

In the foreground you see a sick and very thin gull. He doesn't dare to eat yet, but he will get his turn. Kleew is still a rather young gull, not more than six months old, and he does not realize that he should let the sick gull eat first

One day Kleew had just finished a very good meal when he saw in the distance a big, dark bird. It was coming straight toward him. Kleew was scared. He thought, "That fellow means business! I don't trust him at all. What does he want from me? I had better get out of his way for I don't like trouble."

And away he flew. But the stranger followed him at once. Kleew was really frightened. He flew and flew, turning left and right and up and down but the stranger gained and even tried to peck him. It was a wild and terrible chase and Kleew had never in his life been so frightened. So frightened was he that he dropped the delicious fish he had just caught. The stranger saw the fish and at once stopped chasing Kleew. He went off after the fish and to Kleew's amazement began to eat it. So that was the business he was after.

22

That evening Kleew found a quiet part of the beach to sleep on. It was near the Hook of Holland and when night came the lighthouse light went on. Kleew rested on one leg and put his bill under his back feathers. Before long he was dreaming that he was feasting on the dolphin again.

An old gull at his side said to him, "Are you a good flyer, Kleew?"

"Oh I don't know," answered Kleew.

The old gull said, "Well, you ought to join us some day when we go as high as we can. That's great fun; you can see the other side of the sea."

That sounded exciting for Kleew had never tried to fly that high. Then he woke up. It was only a dream! Then he began to wonder if perhaps he could really fly that far. He decided to try it as soon as the weather was clear.

One very fine day, when the sun was shining brightly, Kleew started on his great flight. He wanted to see the whole sea from the sky. He soared higher and higher, everything on the ground seemed to become very small. The sand dunes look just like worms' borrows. Three children who were playing on the beach looked like little black ants or even smaller. Kleew could only just see them and they could not see him at all.

Finally Kleew went up so high that he really saw the other side of the sea. Over there in England were no sand dunes but huge mud flats and green marshes and black, sooty towns and docks. They were very far away and very far below him.

Kleew soared and glided for more than an hour. He looked at his dunes, then at the ships on the sea, then again at the dunes, then at far-away England. At last he thought, "Now I want to go back to the beach." He sailed down as fast as he dared. What a wild, adventurous glide! Just at sunset he landed on the beach and he hastened to tell his friends what he had seen.

24

From then on Kleew loved to go on long trips. He loved to use his wings and to sail high above the sea. On one of these trips he saw a flock of gulls flying around a small fishing vessel. There must be some-

thing to eat. He flew down at once and, yes, the fishermen were throwing small fish overboard, those that were too small to be eaten, at least for the men. But for gulls they were just right. Kleew caught one and took it to shore. There he put it down on the ground and tried to cut it to pieces with his bill. But that didn't work. Then he decided to swallow it whole. Gulls are greedy, you know. See how that whole fish disappears into Kleew's mouth.

Suddenly Kleew felt that he had been eating rather too much. There was an enormous bulge in his neck. He gasped and hiccoughed as if he were seasick. That is what comes of being a greedy gull!

One beautiful sunny day
in March, Kleew was
standing on a mooring post in the Hook of Holland
harbor. He had just had a square meal of fine sea food.
The sun was delightful and it was warm. Kleew felt
wonderful and for pure happiness he began to call and
sing. To his astonishment he heard himself calling
his own name, "Kleew! Kleew!"

The other gulls felt as excited as he did and they all
began to sing. They felt a tremendous urge to fly, and
off they went, calling, shouting, singing and laughing,
higher and higher into the deep blue sky, until the harbor below was only a little dark spot.

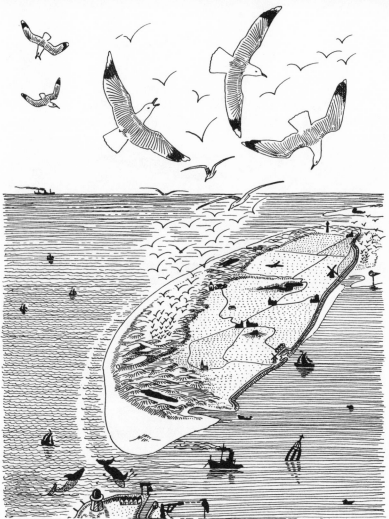

They were going to their own island, Tessel, to their own sand dunes. Tessel is a bird island. There are more birds living there than people.

Here is Kleew's friend, Klia, whom he met before on the beach. They decided to go down to the dunes and make a nest. There Klia will lay her eggs and Kleew and Klia will become a father and mother gull,

27

Kleew and Klia finally found a place that was suited
to a nest and that had not yet been taken by other
gulls. Kleew sat down on the sand, leaning forward on
his breast and wings. He began to shovel the sand
away with his legs until he had made a hole. Klia
watched him with astonishment and with admiration.
In the picture at the bottom of the page you can see
the hole he made, and Kleew's footprints. In that hole
they are going to make a nest.

During the next few days Kleew did not have much time to work on the nest. Again and again stranger gulls would trespass, for they did not know that this lot belonged to Kleew and Klia. When they appeared Kleew always got very angry. With a nasty look on his face he would walk up to the stranger and give him a thorough scolding in the way gulls do. See how he bites the stranger on his wing? "I'll teach you a lesson, my lad," he says. "Just try to get into my yard another time and you will see!" That is how gulls are; they don't like trespassers and attack them as soon as they see them.

Just when Kleew had got rid of the intruder another appeared, Kleew went up to him; he was terribly annoyed now. Very angrily he said, "Do you know, my dear friend, that you are not supposed to be here? Get out or I will throw you out!" And before the stranger could even open his mouth to say "sorry," Kleew took him by the bill, shook him thoroughly, gave him some terrible slaps with his wings. Finally Kleew dragged the stranger for about fifty yards, let him get up, and chased him far away onto the dunes.

All the gulls in the neighborhood now knew that it would not be wise to annoy Kleew. Now at last Kleew and Klia could get down to work and begin to build their nest.

Look at the things they
are carrying to their nest!
Klia has torn off a long
shoot of grass and Kleew
comes with his bill crammed full of moss. They put it
all into the hole and it makes a soft layer as a lining for
the nest. It makes a good bed for the eggs.

From time to time Klia moulds the nest by scraping
with her legs while Kleew brings grass and moss, and
even a large twig.

"But I cannot use that twig, Kleew," says Klia.
"You better take it away." So of course Kleew takes
it away.

Here you see them from
the air, just as a flying gull
would see them. Klia has
fallen asleep, she is so tired.
But Kleew is still carrying
grass. Can you tell which
is Kleew and which is Klia?
Well, have a look at that
funny long shadow of his
and you will know, I am
sure.

31

The nest was finished. Klia was sleeping again and Kleew rested at her side. All at once he heard somebody behind him. He turned his head just in time to see a wicked magpie walking toward the nest. What was he after? Perhaps he wanted to steal moss from the nest. Are not all magpies thieves?

Very angrily Kleew approached the magpie. Like so many of his family this magpie was very bold indeed, and before Kleew could do anything about it, he made a dash—and what did he seize? The long twig that Kleew had dropped the day before, because Klia would not use it. Well, the magpie could do no harm by taking that useless thing away. Kleew was angry just the same and could not stop himself. He attacked the magpie. But the clever magpie got out of Kleew's way just in time and Kleew was not able to hurt him.

Next morning Kleew woke up long after sunrise. He had been worn out by all his fighting and nest-building, and especially by that most·annoying fight with the magpie. When he finally did wake up and looked around, he saw Klia standing near the nest. She was looking down into it in a peculiar way, as if she saw something most remarkable. What could it be? Kleew went to the nest to have a look and there he saw a large egg. A gull's egg! Klia had laid it. How proud he was! Now they had an egg of their own.

Some days later Klia laid a second egg.

And again two days later a third one.

Although all gulls like to eat eggs it did not occur to Kleew and Klia to eat their own eggs. In them Klia's and Kleew's children will grow just as Kleew himself grew inside an egg.

Their children can only grow if the eggs are kept nice and warm. That is why they sat on the eggs. During four long weeks Klia and Kleew took turns sitting on the eggs. They never got bored; they liked nothing better than sitting on the nest. At the bottom of the page you can see Klia sitting. You can recognize the nest by the grass shoot and the long feather.

One day, when Kleew had just returned from the sea, he saw from afar off two people standing near the nest. The tallest of the two was watching Klia, who was sitting on the nest, through field glasses. The smallest of the two children wore a little skirt, it was a girl. They were Jack and Toos, Mr. Tinbergen's children, but of course Kleew did not know that. He only knew that people eat eggs, and he thought that Jack and Toos wanted to steal his eggs.

He flew straight toward them and scolded them in his gull's language. At the same time he shouted to Klia, "Leave the nest! You are so white you can be seen easily. Just leave the eggs where they are. They are the same color as the grass, they wont be found."

But Klia had thought of this and had walked away.

Jack and Toos did not have the slightest intention of eating the eggs. They just liked to watch the gulls. Of course they could not tell Kleew this because he could not understand human language. Fortunately Jack and Toos did not stay long. They went home to tell their mother that they had seen Kleew and Klia.

Before long Klia was sitting snugly on the nest again.

A week later something even more frightening happened. Very early one morning a big reddish-brown animal came walking over the dunes. A fox! He really *was* after the eggs. He went from one hill to another to get a good look around and he sniffed the ground continuously. He walked straight to the nest. Klia and Kleew both flew around his head, shouting

and trying to chase him away. But the fox paid no attention. Then he seemed to realize that Kleew and Klia were excited because he was near their nest. Then he began to search more eagerly and, oh, he found the nest!

He took one egg in his mouth and was going to walk away with it when a man came running down the hill, shouting for all he was worth. It was Mr. Tinbergen. Now the fox was frightened. He dropped the egg and ran away as fast as he could. Mr. Tinbergen put the egg back in the nest and went away. Now the gulls could settle down again—a happy family

At last the chicks were hatched. They crawled out
of the eggs early one morning. How tiny they were!
Kleew and Klia could not imagine that they were once
just as small.

"Now what shall we call them, Kleew?" asked Klia.

"What about calling them Jack, Toos and Dick,
after Mr. Tinbergen's children? It was he who drove
the fox away the other day."

Klia agreed heartily and the chicks did, too.

And Mr. Tinbergen agreed, too. He had overheard
the gulls' conversation from his hiding-tent. Look how
intently he is watching the gulls through his peephole!

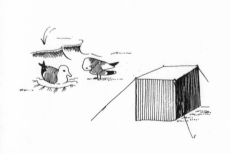

The chicks grew very fast. Every day Mr. Tinbergen watched them from his hiding place. In this picture you can see them all. Kleew and Klia are standing on top of the tent, just above Mr. Tinbergen's head. Jack and Dick are investigating the tent's lines, and Toos has got hold of a feather. Maybe she is thinking of making a nest of her own. The old nest is empty now but the long grass is still there. Mr. Tinbergen is sitting in his tent watching his friends the gulls. Do you see his shoes and his camera?

As soon as Jack, Toos and Dick were able to fly, they began to roam along the shore. There was lots of food — small fish, mussels, starfish, clams and many other creatures. One day when the whole family was together on the beach two beautiful gulls came flying toward them. These gulls alighted just in front of them.

All at once Kleew and the two gulls began to laugh and chatter, for who do you think the two gulls were? Bill and Mary, Kleew's own brother and sister whom he had not seen for such a long time. They were a very happy family of gulls.

One day hundreds of thousands of starfish were washed ashore. A clever farmer from the Hook of Holland said to himself, "These would make good fertilizer for my potatoes. I'll take a cart load and throw them on my fields."

He did not waste a minute and by late in the evening he had his whole cart full of starfish—more than two thousand pounds of them.

"This will be fine for my potatoes," he thought. "I'll leave the cart here for the night and tomorrow I will come back and spread them out."

When he had gone Kleew and the other gulls discovered the load. "That's gull food," they said, and began to feast on it right away.

Look how they are working on it. That's an enormous supper, even for gulls.

**LEEG!!
ALLES OP!!**

The next morning the farmer went out to look at his fields. And what did he see! Lots of gulls! Some of them were still lazily eating starfish that had been overlooked but most of them were sleeping, or preening their feathers. And when he looked in his cart he had a terrible shock. The gulls had not left a single starfish. Look at him! "Gone! All stolen!" he says, in Dutch of course.

The gulls did not realize that they had stolen anything. They liked starfish and thought that once it had been washed ashore it belonged to gulls and not to farmers.

When he recovered from his shock, the farmer could not help laughing. "I should have covered the cart yesterday," he said. "Then the gulls would never have found it."

41

And Jack and Toos and Dick grew up and became
big strong gulls . . . and they laid eggs . . . and from these
eggs hatched new chicks . . . and these chicks grew

larger and larger . . . and one day they could fly . . .
and when they were grown-up, they laid eggs, too . . .

and out of these eggs new young appeared . . . and in
this way it went on and it still goes on : egg—young—

old—egg—young—old . . . and it will go on forever
and ever: egg—young—old—egg—young—old. . . .

Temple Israel
Minneapolis, Minnesota

IN MEMORY OF
SERENE HARRIS
FROM
BETTY JANE BRONSTIEN